Meredie Metz

Happy 1st B'day
we Love Always!
Love Grandma & Grandpa
Tommy & Holciah

This Book Belongs to...

McKenzie Kratz

© Illus. Dr. Seuss 1957

Happy 1ˢᵗ B-day

Love Always,

Aunt Stephanie

Tommy & Haleigh

Arthur learned to read
in school.

Now Arthur reads everywhere!
He reads in the car.

He reads in bed.

He reads
to his puppy, Pal.

Arthur even reads
to his little sister, D.W.

One day Arthur said,
"I can teach YOU to read, too."
"I already know how to read,"
said D.W.

"You do not!" said Arthur.
"Do too!" said D.W.

"Prove it," said Arthur.

"Read ten words, D.W.,

   and I'll buy you an ice cream."

D.W. stuck out her hand.

"It's a deal," she said.

"Let's go!"

They raced to the park.
Arthur pointed to a sign.
"What's that say?" he asked.
"Zoo," said D.W.
"Easy as pie."

"Me too," said D.W.

"Taxi, gas, milk."

Arthur stepped off the curb.

"Look out!" said D.W.

"It says Don't Walk.

You could get hit by a car."

"All right,
Miss Smarty-Pants,
what's that say?"
asked Arthur.

"Police," said D.W.

"And you better

keep off the grass

or the police will get you."

"Bank," said D.W.
"I have a bank.

I hide my money in it
so you can't find it.
Bank makes eight words."

"We're almost home,"
said Arthur.
"Too bad.
You only read eight words.
No ice cream
for you today."

"Hold your horses," said D.W.

"I spy...ice cream.

Hot dog! I read ten words.

Let's eat!"

D.W. and Arthur ran

to the ice cream store.

Arthur bought two big cones.

Strawberry for D.W.
and chocolate for himself.
"Yummy," said D.W.

Arthur sat down.

"Sit down with me," said Arthur,

"and I'll read you my book."

"No," said D.W.

"I'll read YOU the book."

Arthur shook his head.

"I don't think so," he said.

"There are too many words
that you don't know."

D.W. laughed.

"Get up, Arthur."

"Now I can teach you
two words that you don't know,"
said D.W.
"WET PAINT!"